PRAISE F

The Return of t

Twelve Tales from around the Wo

"This delightful collection of stories is a literary analogue to the winter solstice celebrations my colleagues and I have presented at the Cathedral of St. John the Divine in New York City these past twenty years. These fascinating tales, from many traditions, reflect the ancient and universal allurement to winter solstice among peoples around the world."

—PAUL WINTER,
Grammy® award–winning composer and musician

*

"Each story in the collection holds its own magic and offers a pleasant reading experience for young and old alike."

—*Denver Rocky Mountain News*

*

"Elegantly told, [the stories are] an irresistible invitation to curl up beside the fire, cocoa in hand."

—*East Bay Express*

*

"With *The Return of the Light*, Edwards encourages us to shop beyond our own backyards."

—*San Jose Mercury News*

*

"*The Return of the Light* honors the power of storytelling and will enhance the experience of the winter solstice through its stories and fables, ritual and ceremony. It gives us ways to look at this time of year with renewed meaning."

—ANGELES ARRIEN, Ph.D.,
cultural anthropologist, author of *The Four-Fold Way* and *Signs*

Also by Carolyn McVickar Edwards

The Return of the Light: Twelve Tales from Around the World for the Winter Solstice

The Storyteller's Goddess: Tales of the Goddess and Her Wisdom from Around the World

Carolyn McVickar Edwards

Illustrations by Kathleen Edwards

In the Light of the MOON

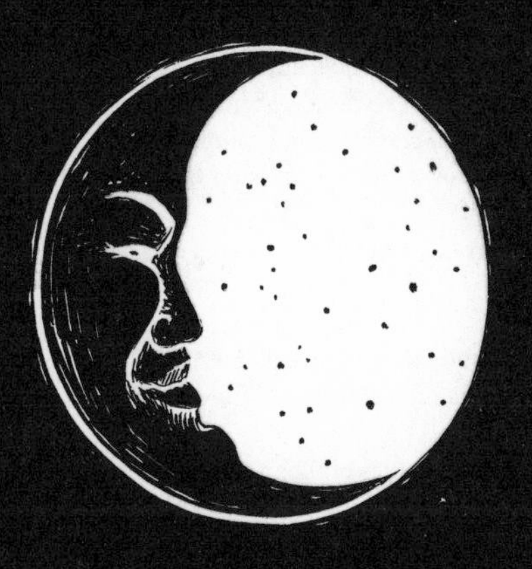

Thirteen Lunar Tales from around the World Illuminating Life's Mysteries

Marlowe & Company
New York

IN THE LIGHT OF THE MOON:
Thirteen Lunar Tales from around the World
Illuminating Life's Mysteries

Published by
Marlowe & Company
An Imprint of Avalon Publishing Group Incorporated
161 William Street, 16th Floor
New York, NY 10038

Library of Congress Cataloging-in-Publication Data

Edwards, Carolyn McVickar.
In the light of the moon : thirteen lunar tales from around the world illuminating life's mysteries / Carolyn McVickar Edwards.
p. cm.
Includes bibliographical references.
ISBN 1-56924-443-X
1. Moon—Folklore. 2. Moon—Mythology. I. Title.

GR625.E37 2003
398.26—dc21 2003059961

9 8 7 6 5 4 3 2 1

DESIGNED BY PAULINE NEUWIRTH, NEUWIRTH & ASSOCIATES, INC.

Printed in the United States of America

for Scott Parker,

integrity through every change

CONTENTS

Acknowledgments

Thanks to Matthew Lore for his energizing vision and audience; to Kathleen Marie, who continues to count lights with me; and to Serena Herr, Mary Ellen Hill, Carolyn Ingle-Price, and Mary Stewart for maypoles, hot bread, and Grandpa's tea.

INTRODUCTION

I'M HEADING EAST ON Oakland's Interstate 580 in my maroon Camry in the fall of 2002. Terry Gross questions a Middle East correspondent on the radio program "Fresh Air." Suddenly, in the ocean-blue twilight over the freeway, the orange moon swallows me. One hand clutches the steering wheel; the other turns off the radio. I stare into her pale gray, peacefully amused craters. For moments, I forfeit everything but gratitude. I am alive.

It's December 1959. My father drives our Plymouth cautiously through the streets of suburban Los Angeles.

My sister and I kneel on the backseat upholstery counting houses necklaced with colored lights. High above, unmoving in the soft, black night, white as my mother's pearls, the moon watches over us.

In 1969, I watch the moonwalk from the cushions of my parents' new flowered couch. Inside the cherrywood box of the television set, the astronauts' space boots mash the moondust around a black-and-white American flag. The three orange globes of the light fixture beside me are reflected in the television screen. Martin Luther King, Jr., and Robert Kennedy were murdered last year. Soon afterward, the family down the street died in a plane crash. Now, in the ninth grade, I am riveted with this new gash in time. But this moonwalk is supposed to be good. I feel, however, not the triumph ringing in the announcer's voice, but a vague resistance to the invasion.

Without knowing it, I have begun the intensely personal relationship with the moon that I will take years to realize. Foreign, delicate, familiar, this night mirror will come to live as much inside me as out.

The next time I meet the moon, it is 1972. I'm out with a crowd of kids after a journalism banquet.

Kenny pulls his station wagon into the beach parking lot. He and another kid disappear down the sand. Miriam and I leave our shoes and nylons under the fluorescent glow of a streetlight and set out in the other direction. Sulky-lipped Patty and her football star boyfriend stay in the backseat of the car.

Cool hillocks of sand oppose my calves. Miriam drifts. The moon hangs, underwear-white, in the navy sky. El Niño's phosphorescent green curls every wave. Possibility breaks over me: I am seventeen. I sprint down the beach, lift off my chiffon party dress, and slither out of my slip. In brassiere and panties I plunge into the silky water. Above me, the buoyant face gazes knowingly.

I return to the car, hair plastered, dress sticking damply to my body. Inside the car, Patty clings stiffly to her boyfriend. Her face is sheet white.

"Are you guys O.K.?" I ask.

"I think you're an exhibitionist," she says. "And I think you think you're bitchin'."

The adult I later confide in agrees with Patty.

I don't remember looking at the moon again until 1982. I am twenty-seven.

In a country on the other side of the world, cut loose from mother tongue and censorial judgment, that whole white face beckons to me again from above a ribbon of hills, promising me something. I don't know what.

Back in the San Francisco Bay Area the next year, an acquaintance tells me about a class called "Equal Rites for Women" taught by Ariadne Weaver (thank you, wherever you are). In the nest of her second-floor living room, we fledgling wise women are fed with chants and candlelight, incense and ritual. Ariadne's hair and skirts flow long. Her T-shirt reads: "I can bleed for days and days and still not die! I am Woman!" We stitch our longings into fabric. We burst free of our fears by snapping yarn that binds arms to torsos. We pass a kiss. "Thou art goddess," we say. Maiden/Mother/Crone: the three moon faces of Eve. We take bites of a red-and-white apple to prove it.

"You're graduated," Ariadne tells us at the end of the second class. "All you have to do now is practice."

So I study and wait. I switch off the motion detector in the backyard. I open the night curtains. I set a chair on the dark deck and gather with groups of women. I ask myself over and over my heart's desires. I live through time and change and loss.

In the 1990s, my yoga teacher talks about stretching through the suffering to yoke ourselves to the quiet inside. At the end of class, he covers us gently with woolen blankets as we lie in corpse pose on the matted floor. Later, desperate for detachment from relationship drama, I begin a meditation practice. Slowly, behind the masks of my imaginings, I start to glimpse the real faces of myself and those I care for.

THE MOON'S PROMISE TURNS out to be a sacred shorthand for all that I stand on. Like the loyal stems of my legs, that changing white sphere scissors me open and closed, holds me to the ground, answers me sure and silent as an animal. My life, like the moon's, cycles constantly from darkness to birth, from expansion to decline and death, then back to the beginning again. The moon is the face I call acceptance.

I feel as intimate with the moon as I do with being a woman. But the moon is male and female, sometimes without gender, often more verb than noun.

The lone moon, like I, begins again and again. Getting up, staying in, going on.

The moon's visage is as marked as mine. By the time a man is fifty, said Abraham Lincoln, he is responsible for the look on his face. In the fullness of time, my blaming and protests have receded. My scars and lately my wrinkles are now nobody's but my own.

The moon, as I do, declines again and again. Deaths, losses, completions. Seasons, projects, habits.

Like life itself, the moon is mysterious and perennial, full of wonder, sad and glad. Like knowing, desire, daring, and silence, the moon stays, disappears, and returns, never ceasing.

The moon is my anti-inertia tablet. Endlessly impermanent, the moon is the ultimate Buddha, the model meditator. Breathing in, holding full, breathing out, and, in the moment of nothingness, everything.

The moon is the master/mistress of entrainment. Steady as a drum, the moon pulls the liquid rhythms of earth and body, and everything else seems to move with her. On dark balconies, the moon quiets hearts and comforts the sleepless. Changing form and costume, the moon has called up stories from every human culture in the world.

Of dozens of moon tales, I've chosen thirteen, one for each full moon in a blue moon year. (Every two and a half years, there are two full moons in one month. The second full moon we call a blue moon.)

The stories are divided into four sections, one for each phase of the moon: waxing, full, waning, and dark. Each section is preceded by a short personal contemplation of the meaning of each phase: origins, markings, cycles, and mysteries.

Each tale opens with a brief introduction to the culture that produced it and a thought-prayer. The stories are followed by songs for the moon, set to familiar tunes, and ideas for group or solitary ritual for every phase of the moon.

So, fellow traveler, come walk with me through the night. Moon is the lantern for our souls.

PART ONE

Waxing Moon

THE ORIGINS

JUST AS I BEGAN to collect the stories for this book, two people close to me got ill, one with cancer, the other with AIDS. My attachments threatened, my sympathies engaged, I lurched into helpless helpfulness. Everybody involved had ideas about options, drugs, diets, herbs, and second opinions. Each of us had disturbingly idiosyncratic views of authority, healing, self-reliance, and community. My need to be seen and appreciated ran headlong into their privacies and ferocities.

In a streak of maturity, I was able to keep my suggestions gentle. But secretly I wanted these attachments confirmed by having these people twin with me. I fantasized myself at their bedsides, lying on my cooling hands. "What would I do without your miso soup, your fresh sheets, that lifeline of your voice?" they would say. No matter what happened, I would remember how essential I'd been.

In fact, my diet suggestions were ignored and my attempts to tidy spurned as invasive. No fairest-of-them-all mirrors here. Proofs of community and purpose went uncollected.

Then came something else, cropping up like a river-bank of grasses. By some grace and good advice, I figured out how to give, not what I wished to give, but what these people wanted. To the one who comforts herself with Christian faith, I wrote of Jesus' precrucifixion agonies. For the one who soothes himself with solitude, I respectfully retreated.

I found a paradoxical feeling of connection in the midst of my loneliness. Yes, it was the butcher birds singing. But out of the blood flowed life. Into my despair and fear plunged the rope from heaven.

How Gidja Kept On Singing

Bullanji People, Australia

Because racism brutalizes victims, perpetrators, and bystanders, mars or ruins lives, and festers cultural and spiritual lacerations, people all over the world were thrilled when Cathy Freeman, the indigenous Australian track star, lit the cauldron at the opening ceremony of the 2000 Olympics. Two hundred years ago, Ms. Freeman's ancestors were decimated and displaced by European settlers. Today the life spans of her contemporaries are twenty-five years shorter than those of their white counterparts. Cathy Freeman's torch seemed to stand for healing. When her fellow First People danced "Awakening," they inspired hope and courage for the ongoing struggle everywhere.

This myth comes from a group of Australia's indigenous peoples. It distills from generations of wisdom and suffering a humorously poignant story of death and life.

Like all the other Australoid First People who sang the world into being, Gidja, in this story, "sings up" his wife.

I BLESS MY CAPACITY TO HOLD
BOTH THE LIGHT AND THE DARK.

How Gidja Kept On Singing

Way back in the dreamtime, before the moon was in the sky, and before death had come into the world, Gidja the Moon lived with all the other Bullanji people near the edge of the Yangool River.

The others made fun of Gidja because his body was round and fat and his arms and legs were so thin.

"There goes Puffball!" they jeered.

"Such a funny-looking fellow!" gossiped the willy wagtail birds.

The kookaburras laughed and laughed.

Gidja didn't like being taunted, but he pretended not to care.

Gidja loved Yalma the Evening Star, and he decided to sing magic songs for her so she would love him and be his wife.

He built a magic circle out of some rocks at the edge of the village. In it he stood two poles—one for himself, and one for Yalma. He decorated the poles with feathers and white lime paint. Every evening at twilight, he sat cross-legged in his magic circle and sang songs to Yalma.

"Dream of me, Evening Star," he sang. "I am honey dripping through your mind."

Yalma found herself thinking of Gidja all the time. Why, she didn't know—he was such an odd-looking fellow.

"Gidja's singing you up, Yalma!" gossiped the willy wagtail birds.

Night after night, Gidja kept singing.

One happy day, Yalma agreed to be his wife. The Bullanji people stopped making fun of Gidja, and danced a corroboree dance at his wedding.

In the midst of Gidja's magic circle, he and Yalma built their bark house. Before long, Yalma gave birth to a little girl. The butcher birds sang glad songs in the trees, and her parents named her Lilga the Morning Star.

How Gidja loved his sweet, little daughter! As she grew older, he began to take her with him when he went hunting.

One day, on a hunt, while Lilga played amongst the blooming wattles, Gidja climbed a gum tree over her head to cut a piece of honeycomb from a hive. Suddenly, a rotten branch, breaking under his foot, struck the child on her head and killed her.

Tears streaming down his face, Gidja carried his baby girl back to the village. The people, shocked and angry, gathered as he walked. This was the first time death had come to the Bullanji people, and no one wanted to die. "Death-bringer!" they shouted. "How dare you!"

Moving as if he could not hear their shouting, with Yalma kneeling frozen in sorrow, Gidja made a little bark coffin. Bent over like an old man, he decided to bury his daughter across the river at the edge of the rain forest.

Carrying the coffin on his shoulder, he mounted the vine bridge that spanned the Yangool River. The crocodiles in the shallows raised their heads to watch. The pelicans on the banks stopped fishing. The dingoes howled.

Just as Gidja reached the middle of the bridge, a crowd

of angry men from the village, bristling with spears, slashed the bridge free from the banks with their knives. Gidja and the coffin flew apart and plunged into the water.

"Help!" shouted Gidja. "I can't swim! I'll drown!"

"Serves you right, murderer!" the men shouted. "You're food for the crocodiles now! Never come back!"

Not knowing what else to do, Gidja puffed himself up as round as he could. He felt himself floating above the strong current of the river. But the crocodiles, grinning, began to swim toward him.

Then the long grasses at the edge of the river reached out to Gidja. Gidja grabbed them, and pulled himself out of the water.

The current carried the coffin out to sea, and Lilga the Morning Star drifted into the sky.

Brokenhearted, now wanting only to see Yalma, Gidja began the long trudge upstream. Toward nightfall, he made himself a firestick.

The villagers saw Gidja's light flickering through the trees.

"Who's coming?" they asked, clutching their spears.

When they saw Gidja, they raged. "We got rid of you! You're supposed to be dead!"

They hurled their spears at him, but their weapons bounced off him as if he were made of stone.

Gidja laughed and laughed.

The men rushed at him, grabbed him, and kicked him into the sky.

Rolling up, higher and higher, Gidja shook his fist. "All of you are going to die! And you'll never come back! I'll die, too, but I'll come back! So will the grasses who saved me! Just wait and see!"

The people on the ground below stood looking until Gidja was just a round ball of silver in the sky.

It happened just as Gidja the Moon said it would. The long, green grasses grow brown and wither. But every time the rains come, they shoot up alive again.

Round, fat Gidja gets thin and stooped as an old man every month. The dingoes howl and the kookaburras laugh. Then Gidja dies. For three days, the sky is dark. But then, slim as a baby's cradle, he lives again just above the sunset. Then Yalma the Evening Star takes her husband's hand. At dawn, Lilga the Morning Star smiles, and the butcher birds sing oh-so-sweetly in the trees.

The Outwitting of Ra

Ancient Egypt

Egypt's dynastic culture thrived for thirty-five hundred years, from about 3050 B.C.E. *through 395* C.E. *In the ancient stone visages of Egyptian people, gods, and goddesses, fascinated modern museum-goers find faces eerily similar to their own.*

The celestial couple Thoth (pronounced Toth) and Seshat together wielded the forces of wisdom and justice. Thoth, God of Science and Inventions, often wore the head of the ibis bird. He guarded the moon and spoke with the "true voice." A few days before the full moon at the start of the new year, ancient Egyptians fêted Thoth. They greeted each other with a dollop of honey or slice of fig on the tongue, and the words: "Sweet is the truth."

To set the worlds in motion, Seshat, Goddess of Writing and Literature, helped her husband play a trick on Ra, the falcon-headed father god. The 354 days of the lunar year divided by 72 (the fraction of moonlight Thoth won from Ra in a game of draughts, or checkers) is about 5—just the number of extra days added to Ra's 360-day year, so that Nut the Sky could make offspring with her husband Geb the Earth.

I HAVE JUST ENOUGH TIME
TO DO WHAT I MUST DO.

The Outwitting of Ra

Back at the beginning of things, the gods and goddesses were lonely. A year had only three hundred and sixty days instead of three hundred and sixty-five. And Nut the Sky and Geb the Earth begged Ra the Falcon Pharoah to let them marry. But Ra, who ruled peevishly over everything, thought too well of his own power. He insisted that Nut the Sky and Geb the Earth wait for another five thousand years to marry.

In a great scroll-lined pyramid, with the scales of justice

at its center, lived another couple who loved each other as much as Sky and Earth did. When Thoth the True and Seshat the Wise heard Ra's decree, they shook their heads sadly. They knew that only the marriage of Nut the Sky and Geb the Earth would bring the lonely gods and goddesses the company of the worlds.

One night, Thoth and Seshat looked out into the possibilities and saw that Nut the Sky and Geb the Earth had married secretly and were holding each other close.

"Now will come children!" they whispered joyfully.

But Ra the Falcon Pharoah was not joyful when he found out that Sky and Earth had disobeyed him. His right eye, the sun, burned blindingly white, and his left eye, the moon, glowed an angry orange.

"How dare you!" Ra shouted, and, just for spite, he created Air.

"Hold those two apart forever!" Ra ordered Air. And Air, a large and spineless fellow, did as he was told. He pushed between Sky and Earth and heaved them apart.

"And, just in case," shouted Ra, "I decree that Nut the Sky will not be able to bear a child on any one of my year's three hundred and sixty days!" Ra clacked his beak shut and strutted with satisfaction at his own cleverness.

"We've got to do something," said Seshat and Thoth.

Seshat and Thoth considered together in their scroll-lined pyramid with the scales of justice before them. They talked and measured.

"If we could just somehow get more time for Nut and Geb," said Seshat.

They weighed their ideas. Suddenly the scales tipped.

"Checkers!" Seshat said. "You know that Ra likes a game of skill and chance."

Thoth's eyes widened. "Checkers."

Seshat grinned. "We'll stake him moonlight."

Thoth slapped the table. "We'll win just enough for . . . "

"Nut to have the time she needs to bear children," finished Seshat.

"Five extra days," said Thoth.

"Let him win most of the time, Thoth. Get him in a winning trance. And, if you wear your ibis head, you'll be bird-to-bird with that falcon."

Ra the Falcon Pharoah agreed to the tournament.

Evening after evening, the two bird-headed gods played checkers.

For three hundred fifty-four evenings, Seshat sat near, tabulating the score. "Oooo," she said admiringly when Ra won.

Ra preened.

Before every seventy-second game, Seshat winked at Thoth. Then Thoth knew to win that round.

When Thoth won, Ra bristled and grudgingly shoved over a portion of moonlight. Seshat put the moonlight in her sleeve and hid her smile behind her hand.

Finally, when Thoth had won five games out of three hundred fifty-four, Seshat yawned.

"You're quite a player, Ra," she said.

Ra flexed his talons.

Thoth stood, swept the checkers into his pouch, and folded the checkerboard under his arm. Thoth and Seshat returned to their scroll-lined pyramid.

Ra seemed to have forgotten his curse on Nut the Sky.

But Thoth the True and Seshat the Wise had not forgotten.

They sat at the center of their pyramid with the scales of justice before them. Delicately, they balanced moonlight on both sides of the scales. Then, chanting magic words, they made five more days for the year.

And so it was that Nut the Sky had the time she needed to give birth: first to Horizon, then to Underworld, then Desert, Vegetation, and, finally, to Civilization and Magic.

And so it was—and even Ra, the peevish Falcon Pharoah, came to agree—that the gods and goddesses, surrounded by these spinning worlds, were never lonely again.

The Thirteenth Jar

Mayan People, Central America

Symbolized by a T-shaped doorway, i'q *was the ancient Mayan word for air, breath, and spirit. Air is exchanged in the lungs. Consciousness moves in and out with spirit.*

In their six-hundred-year classical period (200–800 C.E.), the Mayans mastered feats of architecture and political organization, used the concept of zero, and wrote about consciousness and art in glyphs that did not begin to be deciphered until the 1980s.

Present-day Mayans, who often make their homes in Mexico's Yucatán Peninsula and Guatemala, are an inventive, witty people, famous for their riddles and wordplay. In addition to Spanish, they speak a group of related languages, and have folded their ancient pantheons into Catholicism. In Teotihuacán, travelers can climb the Pyramid of Ixchel the Moon, and the Kekchi Maynas, who first told this tale, still pray to the Sun, Lord of the Thirteen Hills.

EVEN THOUGH MY PLANS GO AWRY,

I TRUST.

The Thirteenth Jar

Kinich Ahau the Sun, Lord of the Thirteen Hills, used to come every day at noon to the forests of Iztamal, dressed in his macaw-feathered jaguar cape. He was looking for a wife.

"Go deep," said the old woman matchmaker. "Go deep in the forest and hunt."

Kinich Ahau took his blowgun and traveled deep into the green of Iztamal.

By and by, he passed the house of the old man who lived with his daughter, Ixchel. When Kinich Ahau saw the beautiful young woman sitting at her loom weaving a rainbow blanket, he knew he wanted to marry her.

"But first, she must see me," he said to himself. "She must believe I am a fine hunter. Her father must believe it, too."

Kinich Ahau hunted for thirteen days to no avail. "I must make this woman believe I can hunt better than this," said Kinich Ahau.

Finally, he caught himself a deer and devised a plan.

First, he slung the deer over his shoulder. Then, waiting for Ixchel to be outside with her father, he walked slowly by their house.

"Look, Father," whispered Ixchel. "A hunter passes."

"Game is scarce," said the old man. "We will not see him again for a long while."

But the next day, Kinich Ahau filled the skin of the deer with ashes and grasses. Slinging the carcass over his shoulder, he walked by again.

"Father," whispered Ixchel. "The hunter comes again."

The old man looked, but said nothing.

When Kinich Ahau came the third day with a deer over

his shoulders, Ixchel said, "Father, he is a fine hunter. Game is scarce, but three days now he has a catch."

"Humph," said the old man. "I smell game—but it is not deer. Tomorrow, you throw water on the path, Daughter, and see how fine your hunter is."

The next day, Ixchel emptied onto the path the lime water she used for soaking corn. Kinich Ahau slipped in the mud. The deer skin flew from his back and burst open.

Ashes and grasses exploded into the air. The beautiful Ixchel burst out laughing.

Kinich Ahau ran and hid.

"I will marry her yet," he told himself. He made himself very small, and borrowed the robes of Hummingbird.

The next day, decked in shimmering green, his head thrown back to show off his scarlet chest, Kinich Ahau hovered over the tobacco flower that had bloomed in one night from the ashes and grasses in the mud.

"Look, Father," said Ixchel. She stepped away from her loom. "Look how handsome that bird is! Will you catch it for me?"

The old man's magic blowgun could pull anything to him without killing it. He used it to stun the little bird, who fell to the ground, moaning, "Swee, swee, swee."

Ixchel gathered the tiny, trembling thing in her hands. Crooning, she fed it chocolate and honey. Then, she took it into the last of the house's thirteen rooms and fell asleep with the bird nestled on the mat beside her.

In the night, she woke in the arms of Kinich Ahau.

"My father will kill me," she whispered.

"Not if you come away with me," whispered Kinich Ahau.

"My father has a magic looking-stone," said Ixchel. "He can see everything happening in the world."

"Give me the stone," said Kinich Ahau. He blackened it with soot.

"My father has his magic blowgun," said Ixchel. "He can pull us back no matter where we are."

"Give me the blowgun," said Kinich Ahau. He filled the blowgun with powdered dried chilis.

Then Ixchel slipped away with Kinich Ahau.

The next day the old man awoke. He could hear nothing of his daughter in any of the thirteen rooms. He reached for his magic looking-stone, but he could see nothing, because it was covered with soot. But then he discovered a sliver of clear space that Kinich Ahau had forgotten to cover. Peering closely, he saw his daughter and the young man going out into the water in a canoe.

Furious, the old man reached for his magic blowgun, but when he put it to his mouth, he fell back choking and gasping. "OchO, OchO, OchO!" he barked. For the first time, coughing came into the world.

Enraged, the old man called for Chac the Rain. "Kill them!" he shouted. "Strike them with your lightning!"

Chac touched the old man with gentle fingers. "No, Old Man," said Chac. "You are angry with them now. But your anger will pass, and then you will be sorry."

The old man pushed Chac away. "Kill them! Kill them! I want them dead!"

Sadly, Chac threw on his black robes, took up his ax and his drum, and flew into the sky.

When Kinich Ahau saw Chac coming, he overturned the canoe. "Quick! Your father has sent Chac to kill us! Dive in!"

Kinich Ahau turned himself into a turtle and headed for the bottom.

Ixchel turned herself into a crab and tried to scuttle under a rock.

When Chac threw down his ax, it hit the crab. Her blood flowed in all directions.

Kinich Ahau swam to the surface and saw his beloved dead against the rock. Grief-stricken, he called to the fish to help him gather up her blood. But the fish ignored him.

Kinich Ahau called to Dragonfly.

"Srrr, srrr, srrr," Dragonfly answered. She collected the blood of Ixchel in thirteen jars. Kinich Ahau left the jars at the house of the old woman matchmaker and promised to return in thirteen days.

When thirteen days had passed, Kinich Ahau came to ask for the jars. "Take them away!" the old woman cried. "I can hardly sleep for the buzzing!"

Kinich Ahau the Sun poured out the jars. Out of the first three came snakes—some poisonous, some not. Out of the fourth jar swarmed mosquitoes; out of the fifth, sandflies. Out of the sixth hummed green hornets; from the seventh, yellow wasps. From the eighth crawled black wasps with black wings; from the ninth, black wasps with white wings. From the tenth crept stinging caterpillars; from the eleventh and twelfth, all kinds of flies. For the first time, all of these creatures came into the world.

Then, in the thirteenth jar, Kinich Ahau found his love Ixchel, whole and well, alive and beautiful as she'd been before. Together, on the back of a deer, they galloped into the sky. There, finally, Kinich Ahau the Sun, Lord of the Thirteen Hills, married Ixchel the Weaver, who became our Heavenly Mother the Moon.

The Tiger's Dessert

Korea

Humans dislike the word "don't." They open doors and boxes they're not supposed to. They populate forbidden worlds. In Europe, people gobbled up wolves' territory. In Asia, they grabbed the lands of the tigers. Wolves and tigers were accustomed to eating small mammals, fish, and the weak members of elk and caribou herds. Crowded and cornered, however, they sometimes attacked the human invaders. Humans responded with traps, poisons, and stories that cartooned the beasts as evil and stupid.

In this tale, as in European wolf stories, the tiger is a dumb villain. The story's mythological outcome shows its antiquity. The ending here is no mere individual family reunion. It is the beginning of celestial light.

I BLESS THE ANCESTORS.

The Tiger's Dessert

ONCE UPON A TIME, before the moon and the sun hung in the sky, people lit their homes with smoky oil lamps. A mother lived with her two daughters in a shack next to a well under a ginkgo tree.

"Dal-soon and Hai-soon," said the mother, "help me make millet cakes so that I can sell them in town."

Dal-soon, the pale, thin-faced elder, ground the millet into meal. Her sister, Hai-soon, the bright-faced younger, mixed the meal with water and sesame seeds. The mother stoked the fire, and the three baked crisp millet cakes for the mother to pile into her basket.

The mother tied on her scarf and cloak. "Dal-soon and Hai-soon, I'll be back late. Don't let anyone but your mother inside the house."

"Yes, Mother. Goodbye!" said Dal-soon and Hai-soon. They barred the door and leaned an ax against it.

None of them knew it, but a tiger, crouching behind the well, heard every word. "Ho, ho," said the tiger. "I've got myself dinner and dessert."

The tiger sprang ahead of the mother, hiding herself behind hedges, until she finally stopped just beyond the bend in the road.

When the mother turned toward town, the tiger stepped in front of her.

"Ho, ho," said the tiger. "What have you got in your basket?"

The mother swallowed. "Only millet cakes, Tiger. You look chilly. Why don't you take my scarf and send me on my way?"

"Done," said the tiger, plucking the scarf.

The mother hurried on.

But the tiger followed. "Good woman," said the tiger, "you haven't let me taste your millet cakes."

"You don't want them, Tiger," said the mother. "Take my cloak and let me be on my way."

"Done," said the tiger. And she snatched the cloak, tying its strings about her striped neck.

The mother rushed ahead, praying she would reach the town quickly.

But the tiger followed. "I do want your millet cakes," said the tiger, and she jerked away the basket. The mother ran for her life, but the tiger was faster. She swallowed the mother in one gulp.

"Ho, ho," said the tiger. "That was dinner. Now for dessert."

The tiger loped back to the little house, where Dal-soon and Hai-soon, chopsticks clicking, were eating rice for supper.

The tiger knocked at the door. *Tuk! Tuk! Tuk!*

"Who is it?" called Dal-soon.

"It's your mother," said the tiger in a high voice.

The sisters looked at each other. "It doesn't sound like Mother," Dal-soon whispered.

Hai-soon peeked out the window. "It looks like Mother," she said.

"We don't know if you're our mother," Dal-soon called. "Show us your hand."

The tiger showed her paw at the window.

The sisters looked at each other. "Mother's hand isn't furry and striped," Hai-soon whispered.

"You're not our mother!" Dal-soon yelled. "Our mother has soft, white hands."

The tiger hurried away, shaved one paw, and dipped it in white flour.

Back she flew, and knocked again at the door. *Tuk, tuk.*

"Who is it?" called Dal-soon.

"It's your mother," the tiger warbled. "Let me in. I'm so tired."

"Let us see your hand," called Dal-soon.

When the girls saw the tiger's white paw at the window, they looked at each other and shrugged. Dal-soon clutched the ax, Hai-soon blew out the lamp, and they opened the door.

With a roar of delight, the tiger sprang inside. The girls screamed. Dal-soon dropped the ax. They ran out the back door and, quick as they could, climbed the ginkgo tree beside the well.

The tiger tore off the cloak and scarf, raced outside and, not thinking of looking up, peered into the well. There, in the water's reflection, she saw the two sisters.

"Poor little girls!" the tiger crooned. "Stuck down in the well! I'll get you out."

Dal-soon and Hai-soon, clinging to each other high in the tree, couldn't help giggling at the tiger's stupidity.

Instantly, the tiger looked up. "Oh! You're up in the tree!" Her tail swished angrily.

Dal-soon poked Hai-soon. "Oh, Tiger," she trilled. "If you want to come get us, you'd better smear sesame oil on your paws and the tree trunk!"

The girls sniggered to watch the tiger grease the tree. Whenever she tried to climb, she slipped and fell. The girls laughed aloud.

"Ho, ho," said the tiger. "I'll get you yet."

The tiger fetched the ax, cut notches in the trunk, and began to climb. The sisters held each other tightly.

Soon the sisters could smell the cat.

Now its yellow eyes blared.

"Something save us!" Hai-soon cried.

Suddenly, a great rope snaked out of the dark sky just in time for the girls to catch hold. Swiftly, the rope carried the two girls into the heavens.

The tiger roared in frustration. "A rope for me, too!"

The rope dropped again. The tiger buried her claws in its sinews.

But this time the rope broke, and the tiger plunged back to the earth where she burst open. Out of her gut popped the mother, who fled after her daughters into the sky. The tiger's blood soaked into the ground, forever after coloring the stems of the millet dark red.

Dal-soon, up in the heavens, with her pale, thin face, turned into the moon. Hai-soon, beside her, with her bright, round face, turned into the sun. And the mother of Dal-soon and Hai-soon, rejoicing to be safe with her girls again, became the morning star.

People still light the insides of their homes with lamps. But outside, the mother and her two daughters, Hai-soon the Sun and Dal-soon the Moon, light the day and the night.

PART TWO

Full Moon

THE MARKINGS

So much of ripening into an adult has been figuring out how to tell myself the story of my life. What is the relationship of choice to chance? What do I learn from the accidents of gender, race, class, and form? Will my scars make me hide or render me handsome? Is the theme resentment or acceptance? How am I sitting with my habits, pleasures, and hardships, and with those moments of awareness that visit like singing birds on bare branches?

Just staying alive sometimes requires courage. I watch the cycle of the breath to find my way to stillness. I'm learning to rely on a soft inner warrior to guard my daring vulnerabilities.

MA-HINA

HAWAII

All over Polynesia, people tell stories of a woman in the moon. Here is Virginia Woolf's A Room of One's Own—*Hawaiian style.*

The warm, water-resistant, mothproof cloth called tapa *(in much of Polynesia) and* kapa *(in Hawaii) is said to have been made first by the goddess Hina, mother of trickster/hero Maui. The islands had no indigenous large, fur-bearing mammals, nor wild cotton, flax, hemp, or silk.* Kapa *is made from the beaten, fermented inner bark of the* wauke, *or paper mulberry tree. Stamped with intricately colored designs,* kapa *was used to fashion sarongs, loin cloths, sandals, capes, bedclothes, and ritual garments for the* hula. *Today, Hawaiians are reviving the art of making and dying* kapa, *which was largely lost to floods of mass-produced fabrics. Women's* kapa *talk, coded in the rhythms of their* kapa *mallets, has disappeared.*

I BLESS THE QUIET HOME IN MY HEART.

MA-HINA

BACK AT THE BEGINNING, the goddess Hina peeled herself bundles of *wauke* bark. She soaked the strips in the salty pools of the shore. She beat them with her mallet on a large, flat stone, and joined them into *kapa* cloth. Like fleecy white clouds, her *kapa* bleached and dried on the rocks. She painted her *kapa* with *ohelo*-berry red and *'ilima*-flower orange.

Hina's hardworking eyes roved more and more toward the handsome Aikanaka. Aikanaka was tall and strong. If

Aikanaka were her husband, Hina dreamed, he would bring her bundles of *wauke* bark larger than anyone else's in the village.

Aikanaka flashed Hina his white teeth. Hina perfumed her night-black hair and laced it with the tiny, white star flowers of the *naupaka* bush.

Hina married Aikanaka. Her *kapa* cloths grew finer. But handsome Aikanaka grew more absent. He gave her children, but he did not cook. He even stopped gathering and preparing *wauke*. He hunted for boar and fished for shark in faraway places. When he came home he complained.

"Why is the water calabash not full? Pound me more *poi*. Bring me more shrimp."

Hina's neighbors began to call her husband "Aikanaka the Wanderer."

Hina pounded away her sorrows on her *kapa* board.

From far and wide, people traveled to trade for Hina's *kapa*.

Many nights, Hina sat alone in the dark. "A-u-we. My hair whitens. I grow tired."

Only when the moon bathed Hina in its cool, silver light could she finally sleep.

Hina's children married. Aikanaka wandered less, but complained more.

One day, after a cloud-drenching, the sun made a rainbow in the sky.

Hina stopped hauling *wauke* bark. She could hear Aikanaka whining. "Why is the water calabash not full? Pound me more *poi*. Bring me more shrimp."

"I am going to live in the sun," Hina announced. She dumped the *wauke*. She hoisted her *kapa* mallet and pounding board. She set her feet on the rainbow and began to climb.

She looked back only once.

But the sun scorched her skin and melted her strength. Her mallet and board fell back into the garden. Hina crawled down the rainbow. She lay in the shade by her water gourd and smeared cooling sap on her burns.

"Why are you lying there?" Aikanaka bellowed. "I need water!"

Hina didn't move. She watched the darkness even out the day. The evening star smiled encouragement. She heard Aikanaka in the distance stomping to the spring for his own water.

The moon rose. Hina sucked down all the water in the gourd.

Strength returned to her limbs.

The moon glowed and bent a moonbow into the garden.

Hina pulled herself up. She lifted her mallet and board. She set her feet on the moonbow and began to climb.

She didn't look back.

Aikanaka woke and saw what she was doing. He lunged after her and seized her foot.

Hina jerked free and Aikanaka crashed back into the garden.

Hina climbed the moonbow all the way to the moon.

There she stayed and we see her still. She is the woman kneeling in the moon, pounding her *kapa*, and setting it out to dry in the fleecy white clouds.

Today, we call moon Ma-hina. Ma-hina is the faraway home of Hina the *Kapa*-maker. We cannot hear her pounding, but we can see her, moonskinned, against the black hair of the night laced with the tiny star flowers of the *naupaka* bush.

The Hare's Gift

Sri Lanka

A student once asked the Buddha, "Lord, are you a prophet?"

"I am not a prophet," said the Buddha.

"Are you a god, then?" asked the student.

"I am not a god," said the Buddha.

"Then what are you, my Lord?"

The Buddha answered, "I am awake."

When he was twenty-nine, the man who came to be called Buddha ventured outside his father's estate, and saw for the first time a sick man, a beggar, and a corpse. Stunned, he set out to comprehend human suffering. At age thirty-five, he rejected severe self-denial as a way to live and instead chose simplicity and moderation. The Buddha taught that human suffering is caused by the wish for permanence in an impermanent world. Relinquishment of craving is the path to awakening. The Buddhist path requires right view, resolve, speech, action, livelihood, effort, mindfulness, and concentration.

The majority of Sri Lankans practice Buddhism. Four times a month, once for each phase of the moon, they visit the pansala *(temple), where they listen to teachings, meditate, chant, and make* pujas *(offerings). On full-moon* poya *days, the whole nation takes a holiday, laying out trays of flowers, burning purifying incense, and lighting small oil lamps for wisdom and enlightenment. May's full moon* poya *day honors Siddhartha Gautama the Buddha.*

I BLESS THE TIMES I LOSE MY WAY.

The Hare's Gift

Once, long ago, a bald moon peered into the clearing of a forest. A solitary brown hare, whose young had long since left the nest, crouched near a rock. She nibbled a sliver of bark.

Suddenly, her ears pricked.

A man stumbled into the clearing. He lay where he had fallen, drawing his legs up close to his body.

The hare sniffed the air, then stepped forward.

The man's eyes fastened on the hare.

"You are ill and tired," the hare said.

"I am tired, my friend."

The hare hopped very near. "Put your hand in my fur."

The man rested his thin hand on the hare's back.

The hare could feel the man's kindness. But she did not know that he was really the Buddha.

"You have lost your way," she said.

"I have lost my way."

"May I guide you to the edge of the forest?"

"I've no money to pay you," the man said.

The hare bowed. "The debt would be mine if you would walk and talk with me."

The man stood slowly. Quietly, talking as they walked, the hare guided the man through the dense wood to an open plain.

The moon shone blankly above them.

The hare looked kindly at her new friend. "You must be very hungry," she said.

The man smiled. "I am famished."

"Please do me the honor of eating me for your supper. I am plump and young enough not to be tough. Let me build a fire so you can cook me."

Without giving the man a chance to protest, the hare zigzagged about, gathering firewood. She built the fire, and when the orange tongues licked up, she bowed low. "Thank you for your company, my friend. Enjoy your meal!"

With that, the hare leapt into the flames.

But the Buddha shot out his hand and caught the hare by her long velvet ears. Once, twice, he swung her around and flung her into the night sky.

The hare whirled, wind in her coat, paws flung open.

Far below, she heard the Buddha call, "A creature as kind as you shall not die! Let all the world look up at night and see my friend, the Hare-in-the-Moon, and remember her compassion for a hungry, lost traveler!"

And so the moon, to this very day, glows around the figure of the kindly hare. Wanderers the world over find hope and encouragement when they see her there.

The Peach of Immortality

China

During the Mooncake Festival, just after the autumnal equinox, Chinese communities pray to the harvest moon. This moon shines more brightly than any other in the year because its orbit has dipped closest to the horizon. On this night, the goddess Ch'ang-O and the heavenly archer Yi cling together again after their long time away from each other. The people in the world below feast on mooncakes daubed with the red of long life, and stuffed with lotus seed paste, coconut, walnuts, and honeyed egg yolk. Rose incense drifts up to the heavenly couple, and bowls of peaches, crab apples, pomegranates, and grapes—never pears, for the word "pear" sounds like "separation" in some Chinese dialects—promise them love everlasting.

I BLESS THE FRUITS OF THE SOFTENED HEART.

The Peach of Immortality

Once upon a time, nine renegade suns burst into the dome of heaven and shoved aside the rightful sun. The nine thieving suns rained down fiery arrows to burn up the earth.

When Queen Mother Wang in the Jade Palace in the West heard the cries of the earthlings, she was greatly troubled. She walked down through the fields of scarlet amaranth blossoms that never fade. She wandered up through the orchards of the peaches of immortality, which bear fruit only once in three thousand years.

When Queen Mother Wang raised her hands and opened her voice, the peacocks fanned their tails. "Heavenly Archer!" she cried out.

Yi the Archer appeared at her feet. He bowed low. The cap on his head was as black as his eyebrows. A quiver of arrows hung from his waistsash. His golden bow sparkled over his shoulder.

Queen Mother Wang pointed to the withered earth below. She swept her hand toward the nine suns. "Remove them," she commanded.

Yi fit an arrow to his bow and—*zing!*—shot down the tenth sun. Then the ninth—*zang!*—and the eighth, seventh, sixth. He shot down the fifth, fourth, third, and second—*zong!*—until the rightful sun stood alone in the sky.

Rain clouds scuttled in. Blue birds fluttered out of the bamboo.

Queen Mother Wang broke off an amaranth blossom and plucked a dusky peach. "Heavenly Archer Yi, I honor you with the flower that never fades. I reward you with a peach of immortality. Eat this fruit when your heart is truly soft, and live forever."

Yi touched his head to the ground. He tucked the

amaranth blossom into his quiver. He secreted the peach of immortality into the folds of his waistsash. Then he strode away from the Jade Palace in the West to meet his love on the banks of the Silver River.

The rosy-lipped Ch'ang-O waited on the leafy bank, stroking a shining rabbit on her silk-garbed lap. The moon opened like a white rose behind her.

Ch'ang-O heard Yi's footsteps. She felt the breeze of his presence. The panpipes sounded. The rabbit jumped from her arms. Ch'ang-O stood. The scent of jasmine spiked the air.

The heavenly archer's bow and quiver thudded to the riverbank. The amaranth blossom dropped at their feet.

Ch'ang-O and Yi fell into each other's arms.

Yi's cap slipped away. His waistsash loosened, and the peach of immortality rolled unnoticed from its folds.

The peach came to rest near the rabbit.

The frogs sang.

The moon glowed.

The lovers finally rested, like leaves on a pool after a rain.

Yi slept, smiling.

Ch'ang-O lay watching Yi's face. When she finally turned her back to nestle against his warmth, she saw the peach beside her lustrous rabbit.

Ch'ang-O reached out. Her finger touched for a moment the delicate, fuzzy plumpness. Her mouth watered. She lifted the peach. She bit into it. The milky sweetness sang in her teeth and poured through her limbs.

Ch'ang-O's eyes widened. Her heart pounded. She looked fearfully at her sleeping love. She folded her robe about her and scooped up her rabbit. Then, trailing wisps of dawn beneath her feet, Ch'ang-O sailed up and away, into the moon.

Yi the Archer stirred. He reached out. Ch'ang-O was not there. Yi woke. He saw the naked pit of the peach of immortality.

The archer's eyes flamed. He grabbed his quiver and bow and rushed to the moon. He pounded his fist at the door.

Bong! Bang! Bong!

"Ch'ang-O!"

The door opened. The rabbit crouched at the threshold, eyes large, quiet, and pink, whiskers and fur gleaming in the heat of Yi's anger.

Behind the rabbit, Yi saw Ch'ang-O. Her eyes were huge, lips parted, face wet with tears.

Yi's heart melted. He dropped to his knees.

The rabbit jumped away. Ch'ang-O stepped forward.

Ch'ang-O and Yi held each other.

Ch'ang-O came to live forever that night in the Palace of the Moon.

"And you, Archer," said Queen Mother Wang. Blue birds fluttered up from the bamboo. The peacocks fanned their tails. "Because your heart, in the moment of forgiveness, was truly soft, you, too, shall live forever."

Yi the Archer went to live in the Palace of the Sun. Once a year, when the first autumn moon is the color of peach and the hearts of the earthlings below are soft, Yi the Heavenly Archer goes to meet Ch'ang-O. We can see her there waiting for him, her long-eared rabbit a shadow at her side.

PART THREE

Waning Moon

THE CYCLES

FOR A FEW HEADY weeks, I plunged into a vivid exchange with a young man I'd met in a discussion group. Despite the actual chasteness of the relationship, I basked in a libidinous glow. My melancholic serenity awoke in flustered joy. I dropped plates. Irises bloomed. I slept less and climbed hills effortlessly.

When the friend withdrew, I waited by the phone. I measured meanings. My digestive system quivered. I reviewed every mistaken choice. And then, slowly, like a garden gate opening, I found on the inside what I'd been absolutely certain had been on the outside. I'd been sure his behavior was causing my feelings. Now I saw my surges as my own turnings more than responses to his personality and changes. For parts of days, I stopped feeling skinned. The moods washed through me, but now, somehow, they were not I. I observed them as I observe my breath.

I saw my habit of being content only when other people's behaviors penetrate me sweetly as the crescent moon or hold me steadfast as the full moon. I saw how regularly I reject all that declines. I heard the culture exhorting me to collect teddy bears and valentines and keep up with my weightlifting. I should always be fierce, vibrant, young. I should give as if designed by an airbrush. There must never be any part of me wasting or dropping away.

Finally, I was able to sit still with my grief. I found it as detailed, in its own way, as the gladness. I found at the center patience and willingness.

The Light Sisters

Vietnam

*The Vietnamese New Year—*Tet Nguyen Dan *in Vietnamese —begins on the first night of the first moon after the sun enters Aquarius. Around red-covered banquet tables, people pray for the safe arrival of the spirits of their ancestors, who wander home on this auspicious night. During* Tet, *everything is symbolic. Feasts are vegetarian for compassion; fruits, flowers, lucky money, and children's dances stand for new life.*

At Vietnam's Mid-Autumn Moon Festival, children march for success in school carrying bamboo-framed, candled lanterns. During the day, they make masks, perform traditional dances, and vie for prizes and scholarships. By moonlight, families serve mooncakes and tell stories. A tale of a carp who strives to become a magnanimous dragon teaches the value of hard work.

Vietnamese myths, first sung during the Hung period of 2800 to 250 B.C.E., *were not written down for another thirteen hundred years. Those later writers, influenced by the rational tastes of Confucianism, often truncated the myths or stripped them of detail. The stories' charms, however, are a clue to the oral wealth of the people who first climbed from the womb of the she-dragon whose husband was a fairy from the great Silver River in the sky.*

EVERYONE IS CALLED TO SHINE.

THE LIGHT SISTERS

NGOC HOANG, LORD OF Heaven, and Tay Vuong Mau, Queen Mother of the West, lived long ago in the great Jade Palace at the edge of the Silver River with their two bright daughters, Sun and Moon.

One day, the Lord of Heaven called his daughters to him. "Daughters, I have heard the prayers of the earth people. They need light to warm their fields and grow their rice."

Moon held her breath. "Choose me," she prayed silently.

"Sister Sun," said the Lord of Heaven, "Each day, you will cross the sky in your golden palanquin."

Sister Sun smiled broadly and bowed low. Moon cast down her eyes and said nothing.

Day after day, Moon watched Sun climb into her golden litter. She watched four handsome, black-haired men lift Sun to their shoulders and hurry away across the sky. She watched the humans below tending shoots of green rice.

Later, Moon watched four gray-bearded men carry her sister much more slowly across the sky. The weeping willows donned green veils. The betel trees were weighted down with nuts. Watermelons swelled. Emerald carpeted the wet, black rice paddies. Moon watched her sister in charge of it all.

Moon's heart ached with jealousy. "She has everything," she muttered.

But when it came time to cut the rice, the Lord of Heaven called Moon. "The people's rice will spoil if they cannot work after dark. From now on, Sister Moon, you shall light the night."

Moon's heart pounded with joy. She bowed low. "Yes, Father," she said.

Moon rushed back to her palace. She scrubbed her face. Her servants dressed her in her most sparkling gown. They hung jewels in every window. They trimmed Moon's lamps to burn like the gold of Sun's palanquin.

Moon radiated rapturously. She saw the people below pointing and squinting, then hurrying at their work. Moon puffed with pride.

Every night, she poured down her glory. Sister Moon was so pleased with herself that she did not notice how slowly the people had begun to move. She thought nothing of it when they dragged themselves about, fanning themselves and lying down in the shade of trees.

But Sister Sun, who rested during the night, did notice.

"You're too bright," Sun told Moon.

"Look who's talking," sniffed Moon.

"The humans can't sleep," said Sun. "They need sleep."

"Be quiet, Sister," said Moon. "You're just jealous that I'm shining, too."

"Mother!" said Sun. "Moon is keeping the humans awake when they need their sleep!"

The Queen Mother rose up out of of the West carrying a pail of ashes. "Girls, that's enough. Moon, come here."

Sister Moon left her post. The Queen Mother rubbed a handful of ashes over her daughter's face. "Now you will shine with a quiet, ivory light." She leaned close to Moon. "People will love you," she whispered. "Even more than your sister." Then, in a louder voice, she said, "Now, take these ashes and smear them on your palace windows."

Sun stood back triumphant while Moon obeyed her mother and silvered her windows with ashes. Moon had a lump in her throat. She knew she was ugly now. No humans would ever look at her again. Resolving to take one last look at the world below, and then to hide forever in her palace, Moon leaned out the window.

To her astonishment, Moon saw people pointing at her and smiling, then cheering!

"You see? I am right." The Queen Mother took hands with her daughters. "From now on, Sister Sun, you will measure the seasons. You, Sister Moon, will mark the portions of the month."

Flutes and drums sounded from the world below, almost as if the people could hear the Queen Mother's plan.

"Moon, you will show when to plant and harvest the crops," continued the Queen Mother. "The Great Bear will be your timekeeper. For twenty-eight days, he will circle your palace. On the fourteenth day, when Bear passes behind your palace, the people will see your full face. When he goes to the right or the left, they will see only the side of your face. And on the last days of the month, when he walks in front of your door, your face will be hidden. Watch, Moon, that he doesn't retrace his steps or linger in front of your palace and cause an eclipse."

Sister Moon bowed to her mother. Then, rising, she looked softly at her sister.

In the morning, when Sister Moon watched Sister Sun climb onto her golden palanquin, her heart filled with peace. For tonight she would shine gently, full of silver for her sister's gold.

The Star Mansions

India

According to the sacred Hindu Vedic texts, Soma the Moon is the swan in the silver cage and the lord of moisture. He churns up the sea; bestows riches, courage, and healing; and causes the watcher to brim with poetry and awe. The milky, fermented juice of a small vine growing in the hills of Punjab (now in Pakistan) is also called soma.

Like the houses of the sun in the Western solar zodiac, there are mansions of the moon in the five-thousand-year-old Eastern lunar zodiac. Each day, for twenty-seven and one-third days, the moon takes a new position, then returns to the start of its cycle. Each of the twenty-seven star formations visited by the moon is said to be a mansion inhabited by a child of the Smith of Heaven.

This story tells of Rohini, the daughter in the fourth lunar house, who becomes Soma the Moon's favorite wife. Her mansion comprises five stars, including the red star Aldabaron. Rohini, meaning Red One, is said to teach the path of Tantric Yoga, or enlightenment through the discipline and ecstacies of erotic love.

I BLESS THE BALANCE.

THE STAR MANSIONS

NEAR THE BEGINNING OF the ages, the round, lithe-handed heavenly architect, Lord Daksha, built for each of his twenty-seven daughters a heavenly mansion.

Some of the mansions had foundations in the muds of mystery. They were the houses of lotus petals and transformations. Other mansions were fashioned like arrows and shields. They were the houses of heroism, austerities, and travels. There were mansions of cookware, feathers, and green chairs. They were the houses of hospitalities and quiet. Still others were mansions of sitars and sandals, snake skins, and songs. They were the houses of the creativities.

The twenty-seven comely daughters of Daksha dwelled in those mansions. They were twenty-seven deer on a hillside, twenty-seven soft-eyed gurus, twenty-seven gardener/warriors, all of them pouring out libations to Soma the Moon.

For it was Soma, the handsome charioteer of the ten white horses, that all twenty-seven daughters wished to marry.

And so it was arranged.

The creeping vine milked out its ambrosia, every plant welled up dewy praises, the rivers danced into the seas, and the wedding feast spun the mandalas of the worlds.

The new husband, Lord Soma, rejoiced. Now, each night of his travels, he would stop to visit one of his exquisite wives.

All was well in the heavens until twenty-six of the sisters began to notice that Soma was staying overly long in the mansion of their fourth sister, Rohini.

Soma intended to be fair. But he found himself longing for Rohini in her scarlet sari in the house with the chrysanthemum doors. He dreamed of her eyes when he was away from her. He remembered her hands, and her tongue behind the white gates of her teeth. Rohini's voice, Rohini's neck, Rohini's feet. Her house undulated rhythms and rhymes. In Rohini's house, Soma's skin shouted for joy.

The twenty-six sisters went to Lord Daksha. Some made legal arguments; others blotted tears and wrung their hands. "It is not fair. He is our husband and we each must be allotted the same amount of time."

Lord Daksha shifted uncomfortably. He preferred architecture to adjudication. "What do you wish from me, my daughters?"

The twenty-six furious sisters were unanimous. "Curse him."

Lord Daksha thought fleetingly of Rohini's happiness. But he was personally annoyed at his son-in-law's tactlessness. And he did believe in majority rule. So, Lord Daksha used his powers to sicken Soma the Moon with the wasting disease.

At that very moment, Soma was with Rohini. At first, he likened the rush of fever to the fire of his love. But Rohini saw his cheeks go gray. She felt his skin grow cold and his hands, limp. In her very arms, her great, shining husband began to shrink.

From the windows of their mansions, the twenty-six sisters watched Rohini race to the palace of their father. Gripping their sills, biting their lips triumphantly, they watched Rohini disappear inside.

Rohini kissed Lord Daksha's feet. "Father! Soma is ill!"

Lord Daksha cleared his throat. "He is ill. And in your house." He cleared his throat again. "Where he has been overmuch."

Rohini stared at Lord Daksha. "Overmuch, my lord?"

"Rohini, Soma has made you his favorite. He has not been fair to your sisters. I have cursed him. Soma is going to die."

Rohini cried out.

Then she ran from Daksha's palace and pulled from their mansions each of her twenty-six sisters. "Our husband is dying," she told them.

She took her sisters behind her chrysanthemum doors.

Soma lay white and narrow as bones on the bed. His breath rasped in his throat.

The sisters' eyes widened with regret. They huddled together.

Soma's eyes fluttered open. He saw them there, all of his wives, and shaped with his mouth the words, "I'm sorry."

When Lord Daksha heard the keening of his daughters, he knew they were not angry any longer. He strode to the house of Rohini and entered their grief.

"I cannot take away the curse," he said. "But I can make it periodic instead of final. Soma, my son, you will only seem to die. Then you will grow strong and full before the disease consumes you again. Let your wasting be ever a reminder that the time with each of my daughters is precious."

And so it was. Each month ever after, Soma the Night Maker stops for exactly the same amount of time in each of the mansions of Lord Daksha's twenty-seven daughters. If, in the house of Rohini, Soma is exalted, he hides that secret in his heart, and all of his wives are satisfied.

The Masks of the Moon

Alutiiq, Kodiak Islands

The Alutiiq peoples have lived for approximately seven thousand years on the Kodiak archipelago off the southwest coast of Alaska. The largest island, Kodiak, is the second-largest island (after the "Big Island" of Hawaii) in the United States. One of six native groups in Alaska, the Alutiiq call themselves the Suqpiat, and preserve a separate identity despite three centuries of colonization by Russians and Europeans. Beginning in the 1960s, after over half a century of punitive language suppression, they revived their Yupik tongue. In 1972, the Alaska State Legislature passed the Bilingual Education Bill, which established the Alaska Native Language Center and officially restored the right of schoolchildren to use and cultivate their native languages.

The Alutiiq are masters of subsistence. Since the beginning, they have built energy-efficient, low-to-the-ground sod houses; hunted noncommercially for salmon, halibut, seal, sea lion, and deer; and gathered clams and crabs. Today, many Alutiiq make their livings as commercial salmon fishers.

I BLESS MY PARTNERSHIPS.

The Masks of the Moon

ONCE, ON THE ISLAND of Kodiak, there lived two girl cousins who did everything together. When they were babies, their parents dipped them into the freezing sea to make them strong. Neither of the cousins cried out.

When they were young girls, they combed each other's long, black hair, and piled the cranberry roots they gathered in one basket.

When they became women, they climbed down, one after the other, into the steam of the bathhouse to purify themselves. Then, silently, they endured the cutting and inking of their new chin markings.

After a day's work was done, they rested together on the beach, leaned against their overturned *qayaq,* and drank in the sky.

It wasn't long before both of them fell in love with Moon.

Night after night, the cousins watched for Moon's handsome face. They giggled and speculated. They vowed to each other that they would share none other than Moon himself for a husband.

One summer night, the cousins lay themselves on a seal skin at the shore and watched the stars ready the path for Moon.

First Cousin sighed. "Moon is taking so long."

"He'll come," said Second Cousin.

They waited on the sand, chewed dried salmon, and teased each other about their wedding night. A misty cloud drifted near.

Suddenly, First Cousin pointed.

Moon was slipping above the edge of the sea.

"We love you, Moon," crooned Second Cousin.

"Come marry us!" sang First Cousin.

The cousins watched Moon climb up the sky. The mists billowed and hid Moon's face. "Why do you hide, Moon?" First Cousin moaned.

Second Cousin laughed softly. "We're waiting for you!"

Suddenly they heard a deep voice behind them. "I am here."

The maidens whirled and sprang to their feet.

Before them stood a powerfully built man wearing a shining, white mask over his face.

The cousins couldn't speak.

"You have wooed me. Now I've come to take one of you home with me."

First Cousin found her voice. "Take both of us, Moon!"

"Both of us love you!" insisted Second Cousin.

Moon hesitated. "I will take you together," he said finally. "But only the most patient one will stay with me."

In Moon's cool light, the cousins promised each other with their eyes. "We will be patient together."

Moon grasped each maiden by her long, black hair. "Close your eyes. No matter what, don't open them until we get to the other side of the sky."

Moon sprang upwards. The cousins felt the ground tilt and the sky fan. Their arms spread; their legs dangled.

On and on Moon flew. First Cousin began to worry. "Will he never arrive?" she wondered. First Cousin couldn't help it. She opened one eye just a crack.

Instantly, Moon let go of her hair. She screamed. She felt her body fall into the night.

Terror pierced Second Cousin's heart. But she did not open her eyes.

Finally, Moon stopped. He let go of Second Cousin's hair. She opened her eyes.

Moon stood quietly, mask in hand, face somber. Behind him stretched a flat gray land cut through with silver paths.

Sorrow and happiness mixed in the young woman's throat. She lowered her eyes.

Moon reached for her hand. "Welcome, Patient One."

He led her to his house.

"All that I have is yours, but one thing," said the new husband. "You must never go into the storeroom at the back of the house."

When her husband was home, it was easy to stay out of the storeroom. But Moon often left to go to work. Sometimes he stayed out all night and slept all day.

The young woman felt unhappy and bored.

"Husband, I want to work with you."

"My work is too hard. Stay here and be patient," Moon said.

One day the woman said to herself, "I shall follow the silver paths and see where they go."

The path she took branched out. At the end of each branch, she found people lying face down, stretched out.

"What are you doing?" she asked one man.

The man did not answer.

The woman asked the question more loudly. When he still did not answer, she poked him with her foot. "Answer me!"

The man on the ground turned his face toward her. He had only one shining eye. "Leave me alone. I am working."

The woman felt angry. She hurried home. "I am going to look in that storeroom," she said to herself. "This is my house, too."

Out in the storeroom, beneath a sealskin curtain, the woman found a set of shining white masks. Some were narrow. Some were quarters or halves. One was round. When she picked it up, she found it surprisingly heavy.

She tried it on. It fit perfectly. But, try as she might, she could not pry the mask from her face.

She rushed back to the house and hid herself under the skins on the bed.

"Wife! I am home."

The woman answered in a muffled voice. "I am sorry,

Husband. I cannot greet you. I have a great pain in my head."

But Moon had already seen that one of the masks was gone from the storeroom. Gently, he pulled away her coverings.

The woman put her hands over her face.

Moon laughed and laughed. "I see your patience wore thin." Then, he knelt beside her, and, very carefully, lifted the mask from her face.

He lay down next to her and put his arms around her.

"Who are those people at the ends of every path?" the woman asked.

"The stars," Moon said.

"The stars have work. You have work. I want work, too," said his wife.

"I see now that the masks are not too heavy for you," Moon said. "From now on, we will share the work. I will wear the masks for the first half of every month, and you will wear them for the second."

And from that time to this, Moon and his wife have shared the wearing of the masks and the shining in the night sky.

PART FOUR

Dark Moon

THE MYSTERIES

So much has changed in the nearly half a century of my life that I feel like a time tourist. Secretly full of questions and contradictions, I appear just normal enough for people to take my money.

I'm as settled with the big picture as perhaps I'll ever be. Yet more than ever I want the details. Just as I finally apprehend how my power as a person and a woman affects others, I no longer command it in the same way.

Death is no longer a thieving killer, but a gnarled gate-keeper. I now read biographies not for models of how to live, but as meditations on all that cannot be known about one person's fearsome privacy.

I'm easier to please. I've blundered so thoroughly, made choices so irrevocable, and felt so tired that any other perception tastes like honey.

I used to wait for nothing with grace. My skin crawled with anxiety during loneliness. But now waiting feels like taking the weight off my feet. My loneliness sometimes so connects me with every other sorrow that I feel a companionship amongst my fellows even when they are not here.

I used to long so much for intimacy, secretly certain I could never have it. The longing was so great, the search so intense, that I cared only sporadically for the physical world. Now a silky, feathered blue jay opens my chest fleetingly, but quite as much as the crush in junior high once did. Now I crush on the nape of a child's neck and the tangle of arugula below my porch.

I have not replaced my longings. But I am no longer in a hurry to slow down calendar pages of days that will never be again. In that unhurriedness, I bear the ineffable with something so humble and undefended that for moments it feels like joy.

The Stolen Moon

Jewish Folklore

Especially before electricity lit the nights, Jews honored the new moon, Rosh Chodosh, *as if it were a monthly Sabbath. The rabbi blew a silver trumpet, sacrificed a goat or a dove, and gave thanks for the renewal of earth and heaven. Women's synchronized bleeding cycles had ceased once again. Men built fires on the mountaintop. Everyone feasted.*

The Hebrew lunar calendar, with its twelve months of thirty days (plus a solar-calendar-coordinated thirteenth month in seven out of nineteen years), schedules all Jewish festivals.

The fabled Chelm (pronounced Khelm), town of fools, is the droll concoction of Eastern European storytellers who lived in harshly segregated, Yiddish-speaking shtetls. *The angel in charge of depositing one fool in every village, they say, accidently spilled the whole bag of fools in the town of Chelm. Ever after, the Chelmites have made us laugh. What else is there to do in the midst of suffering?*

GLOSSARY OF YIDDISH WORDS:

bialy—roll
knish—stuffed, baked dough pocket
kugel—noodle or potato pudding
mazel tov!—good luck!
nosh—to snack

nu?—so? or, well?
oy!—oh! or, ah!
oy, gevalt!—oh, God!
schmaltz—chicken fat
zloty—Polish monetary unit

May all that I have be all that I need.

The Stolen Moon

Two brothers, Fiesl and Faivl, owned an inn. It wasn't a busy inn—folks in Chelm don't have much money to spend. Most of the time Fiesl and Faivl didn't have two *zlotys* to rub together.

But the brothers were dreamers in a village of dreamers. Chelm, more than most places, has its share of people who know how things could and should be.

Fiesl and Faivl weren't ordinary dreamers. If dreams are noodles, Fiesl and Faivl made *kugel*. They didn't just sigh, "*Oy*, would we were rich," and then go on mopping up soup spills and tugging up radishes from the side yard.

No, whenever they had a moment—and they had many, for business was slow—Fiesl and Faivl stacked and restacked their dreams like misers counting coins.

One snowy afternoon, while the two brothers were dreaming of how to be rich, Mendel the Cobbler blew in, bundled up in ragged coats, but barefooted and carrying his shoes in one hand.

"*Mazel tov*!" said Fiesl.

Mendel waved his hand. "Just came in to get my feet warm."

"But you're not wearing shoes?" said Fiesl.

"On a day like this?" said Mendel. "I've got to keep my shoes dry!"

The door creaked and Tevye the Tailor wafted in wearing his hat upside down.

"Keeping your hat dry?" Faivl asked knowingly.

Tevye bobbed his head.

The men warmed themselves but didn't buy so much as a drop.

"Faivl?" said Fiesl, when Mendel and Tevye had left. "No one has a *zloty*. . . . "

Faivl nodded glumly. "But baking," he said brightly. "Baking might make us rich."

Fiesl shook his head. "All day in the heat . . ."

Faivl slumped in agreement. Rich people didn't do long, hot work. But, suddenly, he pointed his finger at his brother. "Fiesl! What makes a bagel different from a *bialy*?"

"The hole?" said Fiesl.

Faivl pounded his fist. "The hole! So we"—he leaned in close to whisper—"have got to find a supplier for the holes, then we sell the holes to the bagel makers in the next *shtetl* and. . . ."

"We're rich!" Fiesl shouted. He whipped his dishrag through the air.

His brother twirled him in a dance.

The suppliers of bagel holes, however, seemed to have gone out of business. So the two brothers settled back to dreaming.

One day, in the month of Sivan, just before the month of Tammuz, just before the Festival of the New Moon, Fiesl was sitting at a table in the empty inn. Faivl was behind the counter stacking and restacking bowls.

Ehud the Crier's voice rang through the streets, "New moon! New moon!"

Fiesl fingered the one *zloty* in his pocket. It was smooth and round like—

"The moon!" he suddenly shouted.

"What?" said Faivl.

Fiesl pointed his finger at his brother. "I've got it!"

Faivl jumped over the counter, and leaned close to his brother.

Fiesl lowered his voice. "This time, no supplier. This thing is free for the taking."

"You're a genius." Faivl tapped the side of his forehead. "What is it?"

"Listen," said Fiesl. "The New Moon Festival comes every month without fail."

"*Nu*?" said Faivl.

Fiesl's voice got louder. "How do people know when it's time for the New Moon Festival?"

Faivl squinted. "Ehud the Crier?"

"How does Ehud the Crier know?"

"He looks at the moon?"

"And where is the moon?" asked Fiesl.

"In the sky?"

"Except when it's not!" Fiesl shouted.

"When it's not?" said Faivl.

"What happens every time the full moon passes over water?" asked Fiesl.

"It stops to take a drink?"

"Exactly. The moon stops to take a sip. And when it stops in our water barrel?"

Faivl seized his brother's hands. "We trap it!"

"And keep it!" said Fiesl.

"And everyone will have to come to us—"

"To know when the New Moon Festival is beginning!"

"Everyone in the whole town will have to pay us!"

Fiesl hestitated. "Well, at least Ehud the Crier will have to pay."

"Not just Ehud!" Faivl shouted. "Every crier from miles around will have to come to Chelm to see the moon."

"Oy!" Fiesl spread his hands.

Faivl spoke slowly and distinctly. "On top of paying us to see the moon, every one of them will *nosh* at our inn!"

Fiesl shook his head wonderingly. "We're going to be rich!"

For two weeks, the brothers plotted carefully. With great effort, they hauled the huge water vat from the front of the inn to the back. They leaned its lid against its side.

Against the lid they set two hammers, some nails, and a length of stout rope.

Finally, on the night of the full moon, Fiesl and Faivl lurked at the inn's back door and waited. When the moon was just overhead, they stood on tip-toe. Sure enough, the moon had stopped to quench her thirst, just as they'd planned. They saw her shimmering in their very own water vat.

In three giant steps, the brothers reached the vat. They heaved up the lid and cunningly clapped it down on the unsuspecting moon. Jubilantly swinging their hammers, they imprisoned the means to their fortune in the water vat. For good measure, they roped the barrel up afterward.

Now all they had to do was wait. The month of Ab would begin in two weeks. Faivl looked at his brother significantly. "Not much more time," he said.

The Chelmites were waiting to harvest their figs. Faivl and Fiesl were waiting to harvest their *zlotys*.

But one early evening, the brothers heard Ehud the Crier raise his voice on the street. "New moon! New moon!"

The brothers froze. Their eyes grew wide. How could this be? It was a trick! The crier couldn't be calling that. They had the moon in a barrel behind the inn!

The brothers raced outside to the water vat. They looked up into the sky.

Sure enough, there stood a spindly fake of a crescent.

"Imposter!" hissed Faivl.

"Thief!" whispered Fiesl.

Faivl put his hand on his brother's arm. "Maybe it got out?"

Fiesl ducked inside for the crowbar.

Carefully, so as not to let the real moon escape, Fiesl and Faivl untied the rope and pried off the lid.

The water was shiny and dark.

"It sank to the bottom?" said Faivl hopefully.

Hearts heavy, the brothers emptied the vat, drop by drop. No moon.

"Oy, gevalt!" Faivl sank to the ground.

Fiesl dropped beside him.

After a while, Faivl fished in his pocket for his one *zloty*. Like a tiny silver moon, he set it on his palm.

Suddenly, Faivl flipped the coin and clapped his brother on the back. "I've got an idea!"

"What?" said Fiesl.

"If we hurry up and make a soup . . . " said Faivl.

"With *schmaltz* and onions?" asked Fiesl.

"And potato *knishes*," said Faivel. "Then . . . "

"When the Festival starts . . . " said Fiesl.

"The people will come and . . . " Faivl stopped, suddenly uncertain.

Fiesl put his hand on his brother's arm. "We'll serve the soup and *knishes* for free!" he said. "And . . . "

"We'll be rich?" asked Faivl.

"In customers!" shouted his brother.

THE TRAVELER'S LANTERN

BRITAIN

The stones in some of the ancient circles dotting the countryside of the British Isles number exactly nineteen. Nineteen is the number of years it takes for any given form of the moon on a given day (say, the new moon on the spring equinox) to appear again in that same form, on that precise day, in another year. Birthdays at the ages of 19, 38, 57, 76, and 95 mark completions of nineteen-year-long "Metonic cycles" (named for Meton, the fifth-century B.C.E. *Greek astronomer), and are said to signal the ends and beginnings of significant life patterns.*

This tale, first collected from a British peasant in the late nineteenth century and found in many versions, winsomely overlays ancient pagan sensibilities with Christian images of the protective, suffering Mary and the cross.

The eery, blue lights of the will-o'-the-wisps are caused by methane gas rising from the rotting plant matter in the peat bogs.

I BLESS THE LADY OF MERCY AND PROTECTION.

THE TRAVELER'S LANTERN

THE VILLAGE OF LINCOLNSHIRE lies at the edge of the fetid, miry ooze called the peat bogs. Up through the branches of the peat bogs' scrawny trees swirl the sly, blue, beckoning lights of the will-o'-the-wisps. Only when Moon pours down her light, the villagers say, true as a lantern for the poor, is the traveler safe from the clawing arms of the moaning, hungry swamp bogles.

One night, long ago, at the end of a month of shining, Moon set out to see for herself the dangers of the peat bogs. Cloaked in black, she descended her dark staircase. All that showed of her beauty was one silver curl and the toes of her silver feet.

A traveler, late that same night, picked his way through the muck with Moon's tiny light for his guide. The bogles cursed Moon's light, gnashing for the chance to snatch the traveler from his path.

"Ours! Oursssss!" they chanted, and suddenly, in the sucking cold, Moon felt about her ankles the grab of icy hands.

The bogles jerked her into the freezing ooze.

Moon fell. Slimy vines pinned her wrists fast. Branches stretched above her like gallows.

"At lassssst!" the bogles chortled.

"Prissssoner!" hissed the will-o'-the-wisps.

The marsh sucked Moon deeper.

The whole world darkened.

The traveler cried out.

The bogles swarmed against Moon's body, shrieking in triumph.

The traveler mistook the will-o'-the-wisps for a guiding light and stepped into a sinking pool.

"Help!"

With all her strength, Moon threw herself back. Her cloak slipped and a small light twisted up from the deep.

The traveler flung himself out of the slime, and ran into the village of Lincolnshire as if Death itself were chasing him.

Spitting, mauling, braying, the bogles pushed Moon beneath the waters of the bog. Before dawn had grayed the skies, they had buried her beneath a cairn of stones.

The people of Lincolnshire knew nothing of what had happened. And they were used to Moon's dark days at the end of every month. So they waited, and readied themselves for her return. They blessed her, jingled new pennies in their pockets, and tucked yellow straws into their caps.

But Moon didn't come.

The nights stayed lightless and the bogles crept closer and closer to the town.

The people tended their fires all night. They couldn't sleep. They heard the choking, sniveling laughter from the swamps.

In the tavern, nineteen men mourned Moon's loss.

Suddenly a stranger amongst them slammed down his mug. "The other night," he said excitedly, "I was traveling through the bog. There was moonlight to see by, then suddenly none. Just when I was sure I was lost, the light came again and . . ."

The eyes of every man in the place riveted the stranger.

"I thought I saw the face of a woman!"

The men rose as a body. "We'll make torches and find her!"

They lit oil-soaked rags about stout sticks. Shouting and stamping, they set out, brandishing pitchforks and scythes.

At the edge of the town, an old woman stepped before them. "Where d'you go, ye brutes? You can't scare the evils with weapons. Ye can't go with noise and lights. You've got to go quiet, feeling your way, with stones under your tongues to stop your whispering. Ye've got to tuck sprigs o' hawthorne into your shirts, and you won't find the lady til ye find the candle, the coffin, and the cross!"

The nineteen men, knowing she was right, did as the old woman said. Quaking in their boots, they tamped their flames, quieted themselves, made their way with sticks alone into the peat bog.

And then, by the light of the will-o'-the-wisps—"There's the candle"—they found a place where a gallows tree stretched—"There's the cross." Beneath it lay a cairn of stones.

"The coffin," they breathed.

And sure enough, a ring of light from deep below lit the black waters.

Sweating and grunting, the nineteen men heaved away the stones. And then, with a great slurching noise, up from the deep came a light, and a face—the most beautiful face the men had even seen.

The men crossed themselves and kissed their sprigs of hawthorne.

Moon rushed up that dark stairway and back into the sky above the village of Lincolnshire.

The people in the town came out, thankfully fingering the bright new pennies in their pockets.

Ever after, Moon has known for herself the dangers of the bogs. Over the village of Lincolnshire most every night she shines, true as a lantern for the poor, keeping the traveler safe from the will-o'-the-wisps and the clawing, hungry arms of the swamp bogles.

River Moon Lily

Amazonia

High up in the Peruvian Andes, hundreds of tiny streams form the source of the great Amazon River. Second only to the Nile in length, the Amazon drains more than half of Brazil, and parts of Bolivia, Columbia, Ecuador, Peru, and Venezuela. Amazonia, the largest tropical rain forest in the world, vast and inaccessible since time immemorial, was heavily colonized during the last half of the twentieth century. This continuing "development" is increasingly understood by scientists and common people to be a dangerous desecration of climate, rich human and animal culture, and medicinal gardens. Each plant, according to indigenous healers, has a "spirit mother," who speaks quietly to those who listen. She tells whether she is food, poison, medicine, or beauty.

The Amazonica lily, called Euryale Amazonica by a German explorer and later Victoria Regia by an Englishman, can grow leaves more than eight feet across. It blooms majestically for one or two days, emits a scent like bananas and ripe pineapples, and gives up edible seeds, the size of a baby's head, that native peoples call "water corn."

I BLESS THE GIVER OF LIFE AND DEATH.

River Moon Lily

Down beneath the blistering green of the forest that reaches along the great River Maderia, which pours into the Mother Amazon; down beneath the flowers shouting mauve and yellow; down beneath the clapping palms, the scarlet banana blooms, the purple orchids, and the thirsty bromelia; down beneath the trunks looped with liana vine; down beneath the giant grasses—springs the snaking, hidden path to the lagoon.

There on the lagoon's black waters spread the flat, prickled leaves of the Amazonica lilies, each wide as a maiden is long. Sometimes, in the mystery of beginning night, the petals of the lilies open themselves: white, rosy-pink arms cradling deep, yellow throats. Listen: you can hear the lily's spirit lilting out her song. When the day is done she will close her throat, pull herself down to her milk-mud roots, and ripen the bounty of her giant seeds.

The spirit of the lily was once a human maiden called Naia who, above all else, loved Moon.

Naia lived in a village of seven cone-shaped huts surrounding a dance ground of beaten earth. In the clearing behind the huts lay a garden that brandished watermelons, yams, peppers, manioc, and corn.

The maiden Naia was the headman's daughter. She was beautiful. She wore her thick, glossy hair burnt in a short fringe. Berry-blue marks accented her cheeks. Her nose ornament shone white and black. The reeds of her apron were tight. Wrist and ankle bands showed off her fine hands and feet. Necklaces of shells, carved deer bones, and tapirs' teeth hung like bees on the honey of her chest.

"Naia," said her father. "It is time. You must choose the hammock of a strong, handsome warrior who will make us rich."

Naia listened to the warriors who came to sing to her. But she climbed, whenever she could, into the trees. For, high in a tree, Naia could see Moon.

And Naia loved Moon, above all else.

She loved his strong, handsome, white face. Her heart swelled when he sang. From her treetop, she spied Moon's hammock.

"Moon," she sang, "are you hanging there for me?"

Moon grew large.

Naia's love grew larger.

"Naia," said her father. "It is time. You must choose."

"I have chosen, Father. I will marry Moon."

"Naia. You are not well," said her father. "You must take the hammock of an earthman."

"I am well, Father. I am singing, and listening. And I have chosen Moon."

"No more of this, Naia," said her father. "You will stay out of the trees."

But even when Naia couldn't see Moon, she heard his song. She searched for nuts and berries. She carried water. She tended the manioc and the corn. And, secretly, she sang to Moon.

She begged Moon to take her up to the sky.

Her father called the shaman.

The shaman drank his potion. He shook his magic rattle and painted the spirals of life on Naia's forehead and cheeks. He sang up her healing and Naia fell smiling into sleep.

"All will be well," said the shaman to Naia's father.

In the deep of the night, Naia raised herself. She slipped into the darkness and began to run. She climbed a tree. She saw Moon, huge and white. She reached out her arms, keening out her longing. But she could not touch him.

And then, shimmering in the lagoon, she saw Moon waiting for her.

Naia climbed down. She ran along that springing, suckered path to the bed of that soft, black pool. She sang out. She dove in.

Naia fell deep into Moon's arms.

The villagers say that Naia drowned in that lagoon. But ever after a giant lily grows there. Wide as a maiden is long, delicate, it spreads the flowers of its arms to the sky. And then, when a day is done, it pulls back under the waters to ripen the giant bounty of its seeds.

Songs for the Moon

Set to familiar tunes

Moon Wish

(Tune: "Twinkle, Twinkle, Little Star")

Moon, I wish I may I might
Have the wish I wish tonight.
By your shifts that mirror me,
By your pearly majesty,
Moon, I wish I may I might
Have the wish I wish tonight.

Lullaby

(Tune: "Rock-a-bye Baby")

Down through my window pours the moonlight
Circling my bed all through the long night.
Silv'ring my pillow, stilling my fear:
She's holding me safely, holding me dear.

Surrender Hymn

(Tune: "My Country 'Tis of Thee")

White moon, my country
Still face of mystery:
To thee I sing.
Jeweled mistress of the night
Glowing with holy light,
Oh, guide me with thy sight:
Sweet surrender bring.

Full Moon

(Tune: "Row, Row, Row Your Boat" from *Small World Celebrations* by Jean Warren & Elizabeth McKinnon, Totline, 1988.)

Full moon shining bright
Shining in the night
What a lovely face you have
Big and round and white.

Moon Prayer

(Tune: "Down in the Valley," American folk song)

Moon, you are mystery, the dark and the light
Fill me with wisdom, open my sight.

Shining young maiden, silv'ry and new,
Open my mind and make my heart true.

Night queen, you're growing: you're shaping my dream.
Freshen my mind and make my will gleam.

Full, round, and milking—with gratitude I
Stand in your radiance under the sky.

Down you are dwindling, old woman so low,
Open my heart and help me let go.

Moon, you are mystery, the dark and the light.
Fill me with wisdom, open my sight.

The Change Be Song

(Tune: "Kumbaya")

By your waxing, moon, help me change. By your waxing, moon, help me change.
By your waxing, moon, help me change. Oh, moon, help me change.

By your fullness, moon, help me be. By your fullness, moon, help me be.
By your fullness, moon, help me be. Oh, moon, help me be.

By your waning, moon, help me change. By your waning, moon, help me change.
By your waning, moon, help me change. Oh, moon, help me change.

By your darkness, moon, help me be. By your darkness, moon, help me be.
By your darkness, moon, help me be. Oh, moon, help me be.

Ideas for Group or Solitary Ritual, for Every Phase of the Moon

The moon is the original equal opportunity employer of the imagination. The moon shines on, whether we're in a group or alone. The moon is in one phase or another, no matter what the date.

Any action on any day can be a ritual—as long as it's infused with intention and meaning.

If I just do my laundry, it's not a ritual. But if I pray for a new beginning with every sorting of color and every push of a button, it's a ritual.

If I have friends over, it's not a ritual. But if we each bring a seed and a pot, sit in a circle, each tell one another what we're trying to grow in our lives, and plant our seeds, it's a ritual.

When I sweep the floor and sweep out overcommitments at the same time, I've made a ritual.

Pre-Ritual—Opening Sacred Space

- Sing moon songs, rounds, or chants
- Sit in, walk, or trace a circle
- Bless yourself or the one on your left with glitter, perfume, water, sage, a kiss, a bell, a hand squeeze . . .
- Invite the unseen powers: east, south, west, and north; God, Mary, Allah, gods, goddesses, guardian spirits, angels, ancestors; pets, friends, relatives gone to the other side; teachers, allies, mountains, oceans, fire, air, animals, trees . . .
- Check-in: brief sharing of what's up with each person
- Stretch, dance

Rituals

Waxing moon—inviting-in rituals: washing, bathing, grooming, planting, cleaning, weaving, making charms, cooking, writing, rhyming, coloring, molding, and carving.

Full moon—gratitude rituals: decorating, gifting, feeding, watering, harvesting, baking, and feasting.

Waning moon—letting-go rituals: washing, bathing, grooming, fasting, scrubbing, burning, breaking, burying, tearing, and tossing.

Dark moon—asking-for-wisdom rituals: praying, I-Ching, tarot cards, rune stones, gazing into flame or water, visualization, meditation, and dream sharing.

Post-Ritual—Closing Sacred Space

- Dance, sing, chant
- Thank the unseen powers you're invited
- Hold hands and say, "Merry meet, merry part, and merry meet again!"
- Eat, drink, and talk

Bibliography

Note: Alphabetical references for stories follow the order of the book's table of contents.

Moon Theme Story Search

MacDonald, Margaret Read and Brian W. Sturm. *Storyteller's Sourcebook: A Subject, Title, and Motif Index to Folklore Collections for Children*, 1983–1999. Farmington Hills, MI: Gale Group, 2001.

General Moon References

Brueton, Diana. *Many Moons: The Myth and Magic, Fact and Fantasy of Our Nearest Heavenly Body*. New York: Prentice Hall, 1991.

Henes, Donna. *Celestially Auspicious Occasions: Seasons, Cycles, & Celebrations*. New York: Perigee, 1996.

———. *Moon Watcher's Companion*. New York: Mama Donna's Tea Garden & Healing Haven, 2002.

Hoffman, Mary. *Sun, Moon, and Stars*. New York: Dutton Children's Books, 1998.

Long, Kim. *The Moon Book: The Meaning of the Methodical Movements of the Magnificent, Mysterious Moon and Other Interesting Facts about the Earth's Nearest Neighbor.* Boulder: Johnson Books, 1988.

Moroney, Lynn. *Moontellers: Myths of the Moon from Around the World*. Flagstaff, AZ: Northland Publishing, 1995.

O'Hara, Gwydion. *Moon Lore: Myths and Folklore from Around the World*. St. Paul, MN: Llewellyn, 1997.

Paungger, Johanna and Thomas Poppe. *Guided by the Moon: Living in Harmony with the Lunar Cycles.* New York: Marlowe & Co., 2002.

Thomas, Robert B. *The Old Farmer's Almanac.* Dublin, NH: Yankee Publishing, Inc., 2002.

Meditation Practice References

Almaas, A. H. *The Point of Existence: Transformations of Narcissism in Self-Realization*. Berkeley, CA: Diamond Books, 1996.

Epstein, Mark. *Going to Pieces Without Falling Apart: A Buddhist Perspective on Wholeness: Lessons from Meditation and Psychotherapy*. New York: Broadway Books, 1998.

———. *Thoughts Without a Thinker: Psychotherapy from a Buddhist Perspective*. New York: Basic Books, 1995.

Friedman, Lenore and Susan Moon, eds. *Being Bodies: Buddhist Women on the Paradox of Embodiment*. Boston: Shambhala, 1997.

AUSTRALIA

Cathy Freeman Official Website. http://www.cathyfreeman.com.au/

Trezise, Percy and Dick Roughsey. *Gidja*. Sydney: William Collins Pty. Lt., 1984.

MAYA

Bierhorst, John. *The Monkey's Haircut and Other Stories*. New York: William Morrow & Co., 1986.

The Breath of Life Symbol of the Maya. From an interview with Heddi Neale as part of her thesis at the Naropa Institute. http://www.angelfire.com/folk/sunflowerfarm/abreath.html

Miller, Mary Ellen. *The Art of MesoAmerica: from Olmec to Aztec*. London: Thames and Hudson, Ltd., 1986.

Ancient Egypt

Aldington, Richard (trans.) *New Larousse Encyclopedia of Mythology*. Paris: Hamlyn Publishing Group Ltd., 1959.

Egypt: 35 Centuries (museum exhibit). Palace of the Legion of Honor, San Francisco, November 2002.

Korea

Choi, Yangsook. *The Sun Girl and the Moon Boy*. New York: Alfred A. Knopf, 1997.

Curry, Lindy Soon. *A Tiger by the Tail and Other Stories from the Heart of Korea*. Englewood, CO: Libraries Unlimited, 1999.

Endangered Siberian Tiger Habitat. Author's name omitted by request on Web site. PageWise, Inc., 2001. http://nc.essortment.com/siberiantiger_raqd.htm

Riordan, James. *Korean Folktales*. New York: Oxford University Press, 1994.

Hawaii

Beckwith, Martha. *Hawaiian Mythology*. New Haven: Yale University Press, 1940.

Chong, Nancy Lee and Janice Lee Baehr. *Raintree Patterns* (quilt patterns based on descriptions of native plants). Pacific Rim Quilt Company. http://www.pacificrimquiltco.com/raintree%20patterns.htm

Kerven, Rosalind. *The Tree in the Moon and Other Legends of Plants and Trees*. Cambridge, UK: Cambridge University Press, 1989.

Knappert, Jan. *Pacific Mythology: An Encyclopedia of Myth and Legend*. London: Aquarian Press, 1992.

Muten, Burleigh. *Grandmother's Stories: Wise Woman Tales from Many Cultures*. New York: Barefoot Books, 1999.

Rattigan, Jama Kim. *The Woman in the Moon: A Story from Hawaii*. New York: Little, Brown & Co., 1996.

Thompson, Vivian L. *Hawaiian Myths of Earth, Sea, and Sky*. Honolulu: University of Hawaii Press, 1966.

China

Aldington, Richard, trans. *New Larousse Encyclopedia of Mythology*. Paris: Hamlyn Publishing Group Ltd., 1959.

Bonnefoy, Yves. *Asian Mythologies*. Chicago: University of Chicago Press, 1991.

Christie, Anthony. *Chinese Mythology*. New York: Peter Bedrick Books, 1968.

Fun Stuff to Know: Moon Cake Festival/Mid-Autumn Festival. June 1999. http://www.geocities.com/Athens/Parthenon/9282/funstuff.html

Li Shang-yin. *Chinese Poetry.* http://www.cs.uiowa.edu/~yhe/poetry/li_shang_yin_poems.html

Mythology: The Moon Goddess, the Hare, and the Lord Archer. http://www.geocities.com/Athens/Parthenon/9282/mythology.html#MoonGoddess

Sri Lanka

Bullitt, John. *What is Theravada Buddhism: A Thumbnail Sketch.* 2002. http://www.accesstoinsight.org/theravada.html

Buddhism in Sri Lanka. Sri Lanka CD. http://www.mysrilanka.com/travel/lanka/religion/buddhism.htm

Hooker, Richard. *Siddhartha Gautama.* 1996. http://www.wsu.edu:8000/~dee/BUDDHISM/SIDD.HTM

McCaughrean, Geraldine. *The Golden Hoard.* New York: Margaret K. McElderry Books, 1995.

Observing Poya Days. Holy Mountain Company, 2002. http://www.holymtn.com/SriLanka/poyaday.htm

VIETNAM

McKinnon, Julissa. "Vietnamese New Year's Celebration Urges Compassion." *Oakland Tribune* (February 17, 2003): 2.

Vuong, Lynette Dyer. *Sky Legends of Vietnam.* New York: HarperCollins, 1993.

ALUTIIQ

Alaska Native Heritage Center. 2000. http://www.alaskanative.net/37.asp

Bruchac, Joseph and Gayle Ross. *The Girl Who Married the Moon: Tales from Native North America.* Britain: Bridgewater Books, 1994.

Edmonds, Margot and Ella E. Clark. *Voices of the Winds: Native American Legends.* New York: Facts on File, 1989.

Green, Rayna. *The Encyclopedia of First Peoples of North America.* Toronto: Groundwood Books/ Douglas & McIntyre, 1999.

Kodiak, Alaska's Undiscovered Destination. Kodiak Island Internet Directory, 2003. http://kodiakisland.net/kodiak.html

India

Aldington, Richard, trans., *New Larousse Encyclopedia of Mythology*. Paris: Hamlyn Publishing Group Ltd, 1959.

de Looff, Roeland. *The Hindu Lunar Zodiac (Nakshatras): 27 Ways to Spiritual Growth* (Tarot Cards and Book). Dirah Publications, Tiburg, The Netherlands.

Martin, Rev. E. O. Osborn. *The Gods of India: Their History, Character, and Worship*. Delhi, India: Indological Book House, 1972.

Rao, Shanta Rameshwar. *Tales of Ancient India*. Calcutta: Orient Longmans Private Ltd., 1960.

Jewish Folklore

Bratcher, Dennis. *Hebrew Jewish Calendar of the Old Testament.* The Voice: Biblical and Theological Resources for Growing Christians: Christian Resource Institute, 2002. http://www.cresourcei.org/calendar.html

(The) Jewish Encyclopedia: The New Moons and the New Moon Festival. Vol. IX, 243–244. http://creation-7th-day-adventist-church.org/n-moon-2.html

Plaut, Steven. *The Wisest Men of Chelm.* http://www.jewishmag.com (search under Chelm)

Sanfield, Steve. *The Feather Merchants and Other Tales of the Fools of Chelm*. New York: Orchard Books, 1991.

Serwer, Blanche Luria. *Let's Steal the Moon: Jewish Tales Ancient and Recent*. Boston: Little, Brown & Co., 1970.

Stevens, Payson R., Charles M. Levine, and Sol Steinmetz. *Meshuggenary: Celebrating the World of Yiddish*. New York: Simon & Schuster, 2002.

Britain

Bang, Molly. *The Buried Moon and Other Stories*. New York: Charles Scribner's Sons, 1977.

Crossley-Holland, Kevin. *East Anglian and Fen County Tales*. London: Faber & Faber, 1982.

Doherty, Berlie. *Tales of Wonder and Magic.* Cambridge, MA: Candlewick Press, 1997.

Estes, Clarissa Pinkola. *Warming the Stone Child: Myths and Stories About Abandonment and the Unmothered Child* (tape). Boulder: Sounds True Recordings, 1990.

Hoffman, Mary. *Sun, Moon, and Stars*. New York: Dutton Children's Books, 1998.

Jacobs, Joseph. *More English Fairy Tales*. New York: G. P. Putnam's Sons, 1963.

MacBain, Gillies. *Celtic Roots: Newgrange Knowth and Dowth: Calendars for the Sun, Moon, and Stars.* Abridged version of talk given to the Sr. Aine Historical Society, Templemore, Co. Tipperary, 2001. http://www.aislingmagazine.com/Anu/articles/TAM28/Newgrange.html

McLeish, Kenneth. *Myths and Folk Stories of Britain and Ireland*. Essex: Longman Group Ltd., 1986.

"Peat Bogs." *World Book Encyclopedia.* Chicago: World Book, Inc., 2002.

Stuart, Forbes. *The Magic Bridle and Other Folk Tales from Great Britain and Ireland*. London: Frederick Muller Ltd., 1974.

Weisstein, Eric. *Eric Weisstein's World of Astronomy: Observational Astronomy, Moon Phases and Cycles: Metonic Cycles.* Wolframresearch. http://scienceworld.wolfram.com/astronomy/MetonicCycle.html

AMAZONIA

Dorson, Mercedes and Jeanne Wilmot. *Tales from the Rain Forest: Myths and Legends from the Amazonia Indians of Brazil.* Hopewell, NJ: The Ecco Press, 1997.

Keen, Cecil. *Amazon Basin.* Greatest Places' Physical Geography. July 1997. http://www.smm.org/greatestplaces/notes/amazon.htm

Kidder, Charlie. *Vine of the Souls: A Closer Look at Amazonia's Visionary Medicine.* The Vaults of Erowid: The Resonance Project. Sept. 1997. http://www.erowid.org/chemicals/ayahuasca/references/other/1997_kidder_resproject_1.shtml

Levi-Strauss, Claude. *Triste Tropiques.* New York: Macmillan, 1974.

Rading, Paul. *Indians of South America.* Garden City, NY: Doubleday, Doran & Co., 1942.

Stephenson, Mike. *Victoria Regia: from the Gardener's Chronicle 1850, authors unknown.* Beaverton, OR. http://www.victoria-adventure.org/victoria/mike/gardeners_chronicle_pm.html

Storm, Rachel and Geraldine Carter. *The Illustrated Guide to Latin American Mythology: Tales from the Aztec, Maya, Inca & Amazon Peoples*. London: Studio Editions Ltd., 1995.

*

About the Author

Carolyn McVickar Edwards, a teacher and storyteller in Oakland, California, and author of *The Return of the Light* and *The Storyteller's Goddess*, is interested in the literacies and languages of earth, myths, books, folk songs and stories, and conversation. More information about her and her work is available at www.carolynmcvickaredwards.com.

PHOTO CREDIT: KATHLEEN EDWARDS